ROLLO IN THE WOODS

BY

JACOB ABBOTT

British Library Cataloguing-in-Publication Data
A catalogue record for this book is available from the
British Library

Contents

Jacob Abbott

Jacob Abbott was born on 14th November 1803 at Hallowell, Maine, United States. He was an American writer of children's books, much loved for his historical and straightforward approach. Abbott spent his early education at the local *Hallowell Academy*, later studying at *Bowdoin College* and graduating in 1820. He then moved to *Andover Theological Seminary*, and on completing his course became a tutor there from 1824-1825. Abbott was clearly academically gifted and soon after (in 1829) was appointed professor of mathematics and natural philosophy at *Amherst College*, having also been licensed to preach by the Hampshire Association in 1826. He also founded the *Mount Vernon School for Young Ladies* in Boston in 1829 and was principal of it until 1833.

After these academic and theological successes, Abbott became a full-time pastor of *Eliot Congregational Church* (which he founded) at Roxbury, Massachusetts in 1834-1835. With his brothers, he was also a founder, and in 1843–1851 a principal of *Abbott's Institute*, and in 1845–1848 of the *Mount Vernon School for Boys*, in New York City. Abbott is best known for his writing however. He was a prolific author, writing juvenile fiction, brief histories, biographies, religious books for the general reader, and a few works in popular science. He wrote 180 books and was a co-author or editor of thirty-one more. His *Rollo Books,* such as *Rollo at Work, Rollo at Play, Rollo in Europe,* etc., are the best known of his writings, having as their chief characters a representative boy and his associates. Works of historical fiction, they recount Rollo and his every day adventures, growing up in nineteenth century rural America. Rollo enjoys playing in the woods, whether he's building a wigwam, setting a trap for a squirrel, or rescuing a baby bird. Yet events don't always turn out the way he wants — the squirrel escapes, the blueberry expedition is delayed by rain and, when it finally does happen, he encounters trouble on the mountain. Yet his friends and parents help Rollo through his difficulties, sometimes by aiding him directly but mostly by prompting him to think about his behaviour and come to a resolution himself.

Abbott had actually preceded these works with his *Lucy Series,* a similar endeavour, but directed at girls. He later penned *Uncle George,* using this character to teach young readers about ethics, geography, history and science. Abbott also wrote twenty-two volumes of biographical histories and a ten volume set titled the *Franconia Stories.* His biographical histories were especially well received, encompassing figures as diverse as Genghis Kahn, Margaret of Anjou, Richard I, II and III, Nero, Alexander the Great and Queen Elizabeth. They were specifically aimed at young people; from about fifteen to twenty-five years old, and within a few years of their publication (1848) they became standard reference works for juvenile history. Abraham Lincoln was even a fan! He wrote to the Abbots: 'I want to thank you and your brother for Abbott's series of Histories. I have not education enough to appreciate the profound works of voluminous historians, and if I had, I have no time to read them. But your series of Histories gives me, in brief compass, just that knowledge of past men and events which I need. I have read them with the greatest interest. To them I am indebted for about all the historical knowledge I have.'

Although the name of his wife is unrecorded, we do know that she died in 1843, after which Abbott moved to New York with his brother. Abbott had four sons, all of whom led happy and successful lives; Benjamin Vaughan Abbott and Austin Abbott were both eminent lawyers, whilst Lyman Abbott and Edward Abbott followed in their father's footsteps and became well known authors. Abbott died on 31st October 1879, in Farmington, Maine, America. He had spent time here in 1839, and it was also the town where his brother, Samuel Phillips Abbott chose to found the *Abbott School*.

ROLLO ON THE TREE BRIDGE

ROLLO IN THE WOODS.

ROLLO AT PLAY
IN
THE WOODS.

THE SETTING OUT.

One pleasant morning in the autumn, when Rollo was about five years old, he was sitting on the platform, behind his father's house, playing. He had a hammer and nails, and some small pieces of board. He was trying to make a box. He hammered and hammered, and presently he dropped his work down and said, fretfully,

"O dear me!"

"What is the matter, Rollo?" said Jonas,—for it happened that Jonas was going by just then, with a wheelbarrow.

"I wish these little boards would not split so. I cannot make my box."

"You drive the nails wrong; you put the wedge sides *with* the grain."

"The wedge sides!" said Rollo; "what are the wedge sides,—and the grain? I do not know what you mean."

But Jonas went on, trundling his wheelbarrow; though he looked round and told Rollo that he could not stop to explain it to him then.

Rollo was discouraged about his box. He thought he would look and see what Jonas was going to do. Jonas trundled the wheelbarrow along, until he came opposite the barn-door, and there he put it down. He went into the barn, and presently came out with an axe. Then he took the sides of the wheelbarrow off, and placed them up against the barn. Then he laid the axe down across the wheelbarrow, and went into the barn again. Pretty soon he brought out an iron crowbar, and laid that down also in the wheelbarrow, with the axe.

Then Rollo called out,

"Jonas, Jonas, where are you going?"

"I am going down into the woods beyond the brook."

"What are you going to do?"

"I am going to clear up some ground."

"May I go with you?"

"I should like it—but that is not for me to say."

Rollo knew by this that he must ask his mother. He went in and asked her, and she, in return, asked him if he had read his lesson that morning. He said he had not; he had forgotten it.

"Then," said his mother, "you must first go and read a quarter of an hour."

6

Rollo was sadly disappointed, and also a little displeased. He turned away, hung down his head, and began to cry. It is not strange that he was disappointed, but it was very wrong for him to feel displeased, and begin to cry.

"Come here, my son," said his mother.

Rollo came to his mother, and she said to him kindly,

"You have done wrong now twice this morning; you have neglected your duty of reading, and now you are out of humor with me because I require you to attend to it. Now it is *my* duty not to yield to such feelings as you have now, but to punish them. So I must say that, instead of a quarter of an hour, you must wait *half* an hour, before you go out with Jonas."

Rollo stood silent a minute,—he perceived that he had done wrong, and was sorry. He did not know how he could find Jonas in the woods, but he did not say any thing about that then. He only asked his mother what he must do for the half hour. She said he must read a quarter of an hour, and the rest of the time he might do as he pleased.

So Rollo took his book, and went out and sat down upon the platform, and began to read aloud. When he had finished one page, which usually took a quarter of an hour, he went in to ask his mother what time it was. She looked at the clock, and told him he had been reading seventeen minutes.

"Is seventeen minutes more than a quarter of an hour, or not so much?" asked Rollo.

"It is more;—*fifteen* minutes is a quarter of an hour. Now you may do what you please till the other quarter has elapsed."

Rollo thought he would go and read more. It is true he was tired; but he was sorry he had done wrong, and he thought that if he read more than he was obliged to, his mother would see that he was penitent, and that he acquiesced in his punishment.

So he went on reading, and the rest of the half hour passed away very quickly. In fact, his mother came out before he got up from his reading, to tell him it was time for him to go. She said she was very glad he had submitted pleasantly to his punishment, and she gave him something wrapped up in a paper.

"Keep this till you get a little tired of play, down there, and then sit down on a log and open it."

Rollo wondered what it was. He took it gladly, and began to go. But in a minute he turned round and said,

"But how shall I find Jonas?"

"What is he doing?" said his mother.

"He said he was going to clear up some land."

"Then you will hear his axe. Go down to the edge of the woods and listen, and when you hear him, call him. But you must not go into the woods unless you hear him."

BRIDGE BUILDING

Rollo went on, down the green lane, till he came to the turn-stile, and then went through into the field. He then followed a winding path until he came to the edge of the trees, and there stopped to listen.

He heard the brook gurgling along over the stones, and that was all at first; but presently he began to hear the strokes of an axe. He called out as loud as he could,

"Jonas! Jonas!"

But Jonas did not hear.

Then he walked along the edge of the woods till he came nearer the place where he heard the axe. He found here a little opening among the trees and bushes, so that he could look in. He saw the brook, and over beyond it, on the opposite bank, was Jonas, cutting down a small tree.

So Rollo walked on until he came to the brook, and then asked Jonas how he should get over. The brook was pretty wide and deep.

Jonas said, if he would wait a few minutes, he would build him a bridge.

"*You* cannot build a bridge," said Rollo.

"Wait a little and see."

So Rollo sat down on a mossy bank, and Jonas, having cut down the small tree, began to work on a larger one that stood near the bank.

After he had cut a little while, Rollo asked him why he did not begin the bridge.

"I am beginning it," said he.

Rollo laughed at this, but in a minute Jonas called to him to stand back, away from the bank; and then, after a few strokes more, the top of the tree began to bend slowly over, and then it fell faster and faster, until it came down with a great crash, directly across the brook.

"There!" said Jonas, "there is your bridge."

Rollo looked at it with astonishment and pleasure.

"Now," said Jonas, "I will come and help you over."

"No," said Rollo, "I can come over myself. I can take hold of the branches for a railing."

So Rollo began to climb along the stem of the tree, holding on carefully by the branches. When he reached the middle of the stream, he stopped to look down into the water.

"This is a capital bridge of yours, Jonas," said he. "How beautiful the water looks down here! O, I see a little fish! He is swimming along by a great rock. Now he is standing perfectly still. O, Jonas, come and see him."

"No," said Jonas, "I must mind my work."

After a little time, Rollo went carefully on over the bridge, and sat down on the bank of the brook. But he did not have with him the parcel his mother gave him. He had left it on the other side.

After he had watched the fishes, and thrown pebble-stones into the brook some time, he began to be tired, and he asked Jonas what he had better do.

"I think you had better build a wigwam."

"A wigwam? What is a wigwam?" said Rollo.

"It is a little house made of bushes such as the Indians live in."

"O, I could not make a house," said Rollo.

"I think you could if I should tell you how, and help you a little."

"But you say *you* must mind your work."

"Yes,—I can mind my work and tell you at the same time."

Rollo thought he should like to build a wigwam very much. Jonas told him the first thing to be done was to find a good place, where the ground was level. Rollo looked at a good many places, but at last chose a smooth spot under a great oak tree, which Jonas said he was not going to cut down. It was near a beautiful turn in the brook, where the water was very deep.

Jonas told him that the first thing was to make a little stake, and drive it down in the middle of his wigwam-ground. Then Rollo recollected that he had left his hatchet over on the other side of the brook, together with the parcel his mother gave him; and he was going over to get them, when Jonas told him he would trim up the bridge a little, and then he could go over more easily.

So Jonas went upon the bridge, and began to cut away the branches that were in the way, leaving enough on each side to take hold of, and to keep Rollo from falling in. Rollo could then go back and forth easily. He held on with one hand, and carried his hatchet in the other. Then he went over again, and brought his parcel, and laid it down near the great oak tree.

Then he made a little stake, and drove it down in the middle of the wigwam-ground. Then he asked Jonas what he must do next.

"That is the centre of your wigwam; now you must strike a circle around it."

"What?" said Rollo.

"Don't you know how to strike a circle?" said Jonas.

Rollo said he did not, and then Jonas told him to do exactly as he should say, and that would show him.

"First," said Jonas, "have you got a string?"

Rollo felt in his pockets in vain, but he recollected his little parcel, which was tied with a piece of twine, and held it up to ask Jonas if that would do. Jonas said it would, and told him to take it off carefully, and tie one end of it to his centre stake.

And Rollo did so.

"Now," said Jonas, "make another little sharp stake for the marker, and tie the other end of the twine to that, near the sharp end."

Rollo worked busily for some time, and then called out,

"Jonas, it is done."

All this time, Jonas was at work in the bushes, at a little distance. He now came to Rollo's wigwam-ground, and took hold of the marker, and held it off as far from the middle stake as it would go, and then began to make a mark on the ground all around the middle stake. Now, as the marker was tied to the middle stake by the string, the mark was equally distant from the middle stake in every part, and that made it exactly round. Then Jonas laid down the marker, and pulled out the middle stake; and they looked down and saw that there was a round mark on the ground, about as large as a cart-wheel.

Then Jonas took the crowbar, and made deep holes all around, in this circle, so far apart that Rollo could just step from one to the other. But Rollo could not understand how he could make a house so.

"I will tell you," said Jonas. "You must now go and get some large branches of trees, and trim off the twigs from the lower end, and stick them down in these holes. I will show you how."

So Jonas took a large bough, and trimmed the large end, and sharpened it a little, and then he fixed it down in one of these holes, in such a manner that the top of it bent over towards the middle of the circle; then he went back to his work, leaving Rollo to go on with the wigwam.

A VISITOR.

Rollo put down two or three branches very well, and was very much delighted at seeing it gradually begin to look like a house, when he thought he heard a voice. He listened a moment, and heard some one at a distance calling, "Rol—lo, Rol—lo."

Rollo dropped his hatchet, and looked in the direction that the sound came from, and called out as loud as he could, "What!"

"Where—are—you?" was heard in reply.

Rollo answered, *"Here,"* and then immediately clambered along over the bridge, and ran through the woods until he came out into the open field; and there he saw a small boy, away off at a distance, just coming through the turn-stile.

It was his cousin James. It seems that James had come to play with him that day, and Rollo's mother had directed him down towards the woods.

James came running along towards Rollo, holding up something round and bright, in each hand. They were half dollars.

"Where did you get them?" said Rollo.

"One is for you, and one is for me," said James. "Uncle George sent them to us."

"What a beautiful little eagle!" said Rollo, as he looked at one side of his half dollar; "I wish I could get it off and keep it separate."

"O no," said James, "that would spoil your half dollar."

"Why, they would know it was a half dollar by the letters and the head on the other side. What a pretty thin eagle! How do you suppose they fasten it on so strong?"

James said he thought he could get it off; so they went and sat down on a smooth log, that was lying on the ground, and laid Rollo's half dollar on the log. Then he took a pin, and tried to drive the point of it under the eagle's head, with a small stone. But the eagle would not move. They only made some little marks and scratches on the silver.

"Never mind," said Rollo; "I will keep it as it is." So he took his half dollar, and they walked along towards the brook.

They showed their money to Jonas, and told him that they had tried to get the eagle off. He smiled at this. The boys went back soon to the wigwam, and James said he would help Rollo finish it. While they were at work they put their money on a large flat stone, on the bank of the brook. They fixed a great many boughs into their wigwam, weaving them in all around, and thus made a very pleasant little house, leaving a place for a door in front. When they were tired, they went and opened Rollo's little package, and found a fine luncheon in it of bread and butter and pie; which they ate very happily together, sitting on little hemlock branches in the wigwam.

DIFFICULTY.

After their luncheon, the boys began to talk about the best place for a window for the wigwam.

"I think we will have it *this* side, towards the brook," said James, "and then we can look out to the water."

"No," said Rollo, "it will be better to have it *here*, towards where Jonas is working, and then we can look out and see him."

"No," said James, "that is not a good plan; I do not want to see Jonas."

"And I do not want to see the water," replied Rollo. "It is *my* wigwam, and I mean to have the window *here*."

So saying, he went to the side towards Jonas, and began to take away a bough. James came there too, and said angrily,

"The wigwam is mine as much as it is yours, for I helped make it, and I will not have a window here."

So he took hold of the branch that Rollo had hold of. They both felt guilty and condemned, but their angry feelings urged them on, and they looked fiercely at each other, and pulled upon the branch.

"Rollo," said James, "let go."

"James," said Rollo, "I tell you, let my wigwam alone."

"It is not your wigwam."

"I tell you it is."

Just then they heard a noise in the bushes. They looked around, and saw Jonas coming towards them. They felt ashamed, and were silent, though each kept hold of the branch.

"Now, boys," said Jonas, "you have got into a foolish and wicked quarrel. I have heard it all. Now you may do as you please—you may let me settle it, or I will lead you home to your mother, and tell her about it, and let her settle it."

The boys looked ashamed, but said nothing.

"If you conclude to let me settle it, you must do just as I say. But I do not pretend that I have any right to decide such a case, unless you consent. So I will take you home, if you prefer."

The boys both preferred that he should settle it, and promised to do as he should say.

"Well, then," said he, "the first thing is for you, Rollo, to go over the other side of the brook, and you, James, to stay here, and both to sit down still, until you have had time to cool."

The boys obeyed, and Jonas went back to his work.

The boys sat still, feeling guilty and ashamed; but they were not penitent. They ought to have been sorry for their fault, and become good-natured and pleasant again. But instead of that, they were silent and displeased, eyeing one another across the brook. Jonas waited some time, and then came and called them both to him.

"Now," says James, "I will tell you all about it, and you shall decide who was to blame."

"I heard it all, and I know which was to blame; you, James, came here to see Rollo, and found him building a wigwam. It was *his* wigwam, not *yours*. He began it without you, and was going on without you, and when you came, you had no right to assume any authority about it. You ought to have let him do as he wished with his own wigwam. You were unjust."

Here Rollo began to look pleased and triumphant, that Jonas had decided in his favor.

"But," continued Jonas, "you, Rollo, were playing here alone. Your little cousin came to see you; and you were very glad to have him come. He helped you build, and when he wanted to have the window in a particular way, you ought to have let him. To quarrel with a visitor for such a cause as that, was very ungentlemanly and unkind. So you see you were both very much to blame."

The boys looked guilty and ashamed, but they did not feel really penitent. They were not cordially reconciled. Neither was willing to give up.

"But," said Rollo, "how shall we make the window?"

"I think you ought not to make any window, as you cannot agree about it."

They wanted to make a window now more than ever, for each wanted to have his own way; but Jonas would not consent, and as they had agreed to abide by his decision, they submitted. Jonas then returned to his work, and the boys stood by the side of the brook, not knowing exactly what to do. Jonas told them, when they went away, that he expected that they would have another quarrel, as he perceived that their hearts were still in a bad state.

HEARTS WRONG.

The boys sat down on the bank of the brook, and began to pick up little stones and throw them into the water. They began soon to talk of the window again.

Rollo said, "Jonas thought you were most to blame, I know."

"No, he did not," replied James. "He blamed you the most; he said you were unjust."

"I don't care," said Rollo. "You do not know how to build a wigwam. You cannot reach high enough to make a window."

"I *can* reach high," said James. "I can reach as high as that," said he, stretching up his hand.

"And I can reach as high as *that*," said Rollo, stretching up his hand higher than James did; for he was a little taller.

James was somewhat vexed to find that Rollo could reach higher than he could, though it was very foolish to allow himself to be put out of humor by such a thing. But boys, when they are ill-humored, and dispute, are always unreasonable and foolish. James determined not to be outdone, so he took up a stick, and reached it up in the air as high as he could, and said,

"I can reach up as high as *that*."

Then Rollo took up a stone, and tossed it up into the air, saying,

"And I can reach as high as that."

Now, when boys throw stones into the air, they ought to consider where they will come down; but, unfortunately, Rollo did not in this case, and the stone fell directly upon James's head. It was, however a small stone, and his cap prevented it from hurting him much; but he was already vexed and out of humor, and so he began to cry out aloud.

Rollo was frightened a little, for he was afraid he had hurt his cousin a good deal, and then he expected too that Jonas would come. But Jonas took no notice of the crying, but went on with his work. Now, Jonas was very kind and careful, and always came quick when there was any one hurt. But this time, he knew by the tone of James's crying, that it was vexation rather than pain that caused it.

James, finding that his crying did no good, gradually became still; and in a few minutes, as he happened to look round, his eye rested on the stone where they had put their half dollars, and he saw that only one of them was there.

"O, Rollo," said he, "one of our half dollars is gone."

They went to the stone, and, true enough, one was gone. They looked around, but it was no where to be found. Boys that are out of humor with one another, are never at a loss for subjects of dispute; and Rollo said he believed James had taken it, and James charged it upon Rollo. Then there was a dispute who should have the one that was left. James knew it was his; he said he remembered *exactly* how his looked;

and Rollo knew it was his, for the head and the stars were very bright on his, and they were very bright on this. James, however, had the half dollar, and would not give it up; and so Rollo went to Jonas, and told him that James had got his half dollar.

Jonas came, and heard the whole story from both of the boys. James said he *knew* the one that was left was his, for he remembered exactly how it looked, and he also remembered exactly the very spot on the stone where he put it down.

James did not mean to tell a lie, but he was a little angry and excited, and when boys are in that state of mind, they are very apt to say they know not what.

Jonas looked at both sides of the half dollar very attentively.

"Which half dollar was it," said he, "that you tried to get the eagle off of?"

"Mine," said Rollo; "let me see."

Jonas held down the half dollar, and showed to Rollo and James the marks and scratches made by the pin; proving that this was Rollo's half dollar. James looked ashamed and confounded; Jonas just waited to hear what he would say.

HEARTS RIGHT AGAIN.

James stood still a minute, thinking, presently he said,

"Well, Rollo, I suppose my half dollar is lost, but I am glad yours is safe, at any rate."

"I am sorry yours is lost," said Rollo, "but then I can give you half of what I buy with mine."

"Where did you put the half dollars?" said Jonas.

"On that rock," said Rollo.

They walked along towards the rock. It was by the edge of the water; Jonas thought that as they had been dragging boughs of trees along near the rock, some little branch might have reached over and brushed off one of the pieces of money into the water. So he walked up to it and looked over.

In a minute or two, he pointed down, and the boys looked and saw something bright and glittering on the bottom.

"Is that it?" said James.

"I believe it is," said Jonas. Jonas then took off his jacket, rolled up his shirt sleeve, lay down on the rock, and reached his arm down into the water, but it was a little too deep. He could not reach it.

"I cannot get it so," said he.

"What shall we do?" said James. "How foolish I was to put it so near the water!"

"I think we shall contrive some way to get it," said Jonas.

He then sat down on the rock and looked into the water. "We can go home and get a long pair of tongs, and get it with them at any rate," said he.

"O, yes," said Rollo, "I will go and get them;" and he ran off towards the bridge.

"No," said Jonas, "stop; I will try one plan more."

So he went and cut a long straight stem of a bush, and trimmed it up smooth, and cut the largest end off exactly square. Then he went to a hemlock tree near, and took off some of the gum, which was very "sticky." He pressed some of this with his knife on the end of the stick. Then he reached it very carefully down, and pressed it hard against the half dollar; it crowded the half dollar down into the sand, out of sight.

"There, you have lost it," said James.

"I don't know," said Jonas; and he began slowly and carefully to draw it up.

When the end of the stick came up out of the sand, the boys saw, to their great delight, that the half dollar was sticking fast on. They clapped their hands, and capered about on the stone, while Jonas gently drew up the half dollar, and put it, all wet and dripping, into James's hands.

The boys thanked Jonas for getting up the money, and then they asked him to keep both pieces for them until they went home. Then they began to think of the wigwam again.

"We will make the window as you want it, James," said Rollo; "I am willing."

"No," said James, "I was just going to say we would make it your way. I rather think it would be better to make it towards the land."

"Why can you not have two windows?" said Jonas.

"So we can," said both of the boys; and they immediately went to work collecting branches and weaving them in, leaving a space for a window both sides. Their quarrelsome feelings were all gone, and they talked very pleasantly at their work until it was time for them to go home to dinner.

www.ingramcontent.com/pod-product-compliance
Lightning Source LLC
Chambersburg PA
CBHW030243180626
46810CB00008B/3263